THE WAY HOME

by Judith Benét Richardson · pictures by Salley Mavor

Macmillan Publishing Company   New York

Collier Macmillan Canada   Toronto

Maxwell Macmillan International Publishing Group

New York   Oxford   Singapore   Sydney

To Peter and Ian
(and for Molly and Judy-Sue)

10   9   8   7   6   5   4   3   2

Library of Congress Cataloging-in-Publication Data • Richardson, Judith Benét, date. • The way home/by Judith Benét Richardson; pictures by Salley Mavor. — 1st American ed.   p.   cm. Summary: Unable to convince her baby to leave the beach where they have spent the day playing, a mother elephant uses inventive means to draw her young one away to home and safety. [1. Elephants — Fiction.] I. Mavor, Salley, ill. II. Title. PZ7.R3949Way 1991   [E] — dc 19   88-35951 CIP AC   I S B N 0 - 0 2 - 7 7 6 1 4 5 - 2

Savi went down to the beach with her mother.

They splashed and rolled in the water.
Then Savi played with her boat.

Her mother cooled off in the shade
of a banana tree and ate bananas.
She rolled her big body from side to side
in the sand.
Savi stayed in the water.

The hot sun slid down and made long shadows
stretch out in front of the banana trees.

"Now it's time to go home," rumbled
Savi's mother.
 Savi sucked in another trunkful of water.

"Time to go home," grumbled her mother, more loudly.

Savi squirted water into her boat to see if it would sink.

"*Time to go home,*" trumpeted her mother.

"No, no, no," squealed Savi, waving her trunk back and forth. "No, no, no."

And she stayed as far out in the water as she could.

Her mother stamped her feet and trumpeted, but Savi did not come.

So the big elephant turned around and walked off
through the long shadows of the banana trees.

The sun went down a little farther.

Savi came out of the water and lay on her towel.

She began to feel cold and hungry.

A star appeared in the sky.
Then Savi saw a pale shape in the grass.
Was it the new moon lying there?
Was it an elephant's toenail?
No, it was a banana.

Savi picked it up. As she did, she saw
another banana just beyond the first banana . . .

and beyond it another, and
beyond that still another.

Savi followed the banana trail,
eating as she went.

When she got to the end of the trail, and all
the bananas were gone, there was her mother!
Savi ran to her.

Savi looked up and saw, high over her mother's head, one last banana.

She stretched and stretched her trunk, but she could not reach it.

"Please pick the last banana for me," she said.

"That banana is the moon," said her mother. "It will help us to see our way home."

Savi curled her trunk around her mother's tail,
and they went home through the trees.

The original pictures for this book were made in fabric relief. This art form includes many techniques, including appliqué, embroidery, wrapping, dyeing, and soft sculpture.

The background fabric was dyed and then sewn together. Three-dimensional pieces were made from a variety of materials, including covered and stuffed cardboard shapes, wrapped wire, found objects, and fabric. Details were embroidered onto the shapes and background and then the three-dimensional pieces were sewn into place. All stitching was done by hand.

The artwork was then made into color transparencies by Gamma One Conversions, Inc., and reproduced in full color.

The text of the book was set in 18 point Simoncini Garamond by TDC Laserimages. The book was printed and bound by Toppan Printing Co. (America), Inc., in Hong Kong.

E   Richardson, Judith
RIC   Benet

        The way home

$13.95

DATE		
APR 29 '94		MAR 1 2 '98
MAY 18 '94	MAY 06 '97	
NOV 0 1 '94		APR 0 7 1998
DEC 1 8 '95	MAY 2 1 '97	MAY 0 5 1998
DEC 19 '95	MAY 2 1 '97	
FEB 0 9 '96	SEP 2 3 '97	
MAR 0 7 '96	NOV 1 8 '97	JUN 0 1 '9
OCT 1 0 '96		
	DEC 1 6 '97	
MAR 3 1 '98	DEC 2 3 '97	

© THE BAKER & TAYLOR CO.